Adapted by Barbara Winthrop

Illustrated by Pilot Studio

 A GOLDEN BOOK • NEW YORK

rhcbooks.com

ISBN 978-0-7364-3875-9 (trade) — ISBN 978-0-7364-3876-6 (ebook)

Printed in the United States of America

10 9 8 7 6 5 4 3 2 1

There once was a young man named **Han Solo** who lived on the planet Corellia.

Han worked for a wormlike gangster named Lady Proxima, but he longed to escape and fly among the stars. So he stole a speeder and some valuable fuel called coaxium. But he couldn't leave the planet without his best friend, **Qi'ra**.

Han had to rescue Qi'ra from Lady Proxima's dark, watery den. He didn't have a blaster, but he had a plan . . . and a rock. **SMASH!**

Han shattered a window and sunlight streamed into the den, causing the evil Lady Proxima to dive underwater.

Han and Qi'ra raced toward the local spaceport. But just when it seemed that they were going to get away, Qi'ra was **captured** by Lady Proxima's guards!

"Go!" Qi'ra shouted to Han. "Run!"

Han was alone and didn't know what to do. So he joined the Imperial Navy to get off Corellia and become a pilot.

But things didn't go as Han planned. He ended up having to fight for the evil Empire as a foot soldier.

One day, on a muddly battlefield, Han met a disguised smuggler named **Beckett**. The smuggler and his crew were stealing a big ship called an AT-hauler from the Empire. Han asked if he could come along, but Beckett didn't think the young man was up to the challenge.

Instead, Beckett told an Imperial commander that Han was trying to run away!

"Feed him to the beast," the commander ordered.

Han was thrown into a pit with a **giant furry creature**!

Luckily, the creature wasn't a monster. He was a friendly **Wookiee** named **Chewbacca**!

Han and Chewbacca worked together to **escape**!
Soon they found Beckett and joined the rest of his crew:
Val the smuggler and a four-armed pilot named **Rio**.

Han and Chewbacca's **first mission** with
Beckett's crew was to steal fuel from an Imperial train.

But they weren't the only ones trying to rob the Empire's train. The fearsome warrior **Enfys Nest** and a gang of masked bandits wanted the valuable fuel, too.

It was time for a **fight**!

Unfortunately, the mission went horribly wrong! Val and Rio didn't make it through, and the train car holding the fuel **crashed** into the side of a mountain. Luckily, Han took control of the AT-hauler and flew Chewbacca and Beckett to safety just in time.

But Beckett was in trouble. The fuel was for **Dryden Vos**—the leader of a gang called Crimson Dawn. Now he, Han, and Chewbacca had to tell Vos they had failed.

On board Dryden's fancy ship, Han asked the crime lord to give them another chance.

Vos agreed, under one condition: they take his top officer with them. It was **Qi'ra**!

Together again, Han and Qi'ra came up with a new plan. They would steal the fuel from the mining planet of Kessel.

To complete the mission, they'd need a fast ship. Qi'ra knew the perfect one: the **Millennium Falcon**!

Han tried to win the *Falcon* from its owner, **Lando Calrissian**, in a game called sabacc. But Lando cheated!

Qi'ra offered Lando a share in the profits from the stolen fuel. Lando agreed to fly them to Kessel, along with his droid copilot, **L3-37**. L3 was the best navigator in the galaxy. She would take the ship safely through a **dangerous** space storm called the Maelstrom that surrounded Kessel.

Soon the *Falcon* landed on Kessel. Han **snuck** deep into the Kessel mine. While Han stole the fuel, Chewbacca and L3-37 set some captured Wookiees and droids free.

Qi'ra, Lando, Beckett, and the Wookiees held off the mine guards as Han and Chewbacca loaded the fuel onto the *Falcon*.

The team blasted off, but an **Imperial Star Destroyer** blocked their path! Lando and L3-37 were injured, so Han took the controls and piloted the *Falcon* on a different route through the Maelstrom.

Little did the crew know that a **giant beast** lived inside the Maelstrom!

Thinking fast, Han launched the *Falcon*'s escape pod to distract the beast. Then he used a burst of the stolen fuel to **zoom away**! Han piloted a course for the planet of Savareen to deliver the fuel to Dryden.

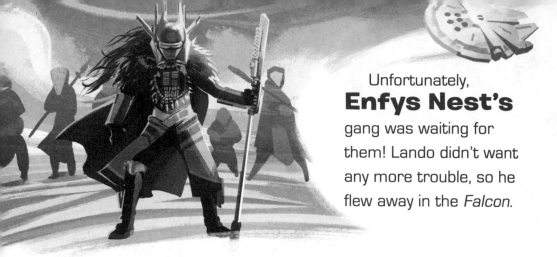

Unfortunately, **Enfys Nest's** gang was waiting for them! Lando didn't want any more trouble, so he flew away in the *Falcon*.

Han was **shocked** when Enfys removed her mask, revealing the face of a young woman. Enfys wasn't an enemy. She needed the fuel to fight against Dryden's evil gang and the Empire.

Han and Qi'ra wanted to help Enfys, so they tried to trick Dryden. But the crime lord had been warned . . . by Beckett!

With no other choice, Qi'ra and Han sprang into **action** and defeated Dryden. Beckett ran off with all the fuel—and took Chewbacca with him!

Han went after Beckett to save Chewie. He hoped Qi'ra would meet up with him soon.

Instead, Qi'ra pledged her loyalty to Crimson Dawn's leader: Darth Maul.

Meanwhile, Han found Beckett. They both drew their blasters, but Han was a little quicker.

Han gave the fuel to Enfys. To thank him for his help, she gave him one vial of the valuable fuel. With Chewbacca at his side, Han tracked down Lando for another game of sabacc.

"I'm feeling pretty **lucky** tonight," Han said. Lando wouldn't cheat him out of his prize again!

Han finally won the *Millennium Falcon* from Lando. He took his place in the captain's chair, with Chewbacca seated beside him. The two friends smiled at the **galaxy of possibilities** that stretched out before them. . . .